THE KING'S HATS

SHEILA MAY BIRD

Illustrated by Mark Beech

WELBECK
FLAME

The King put on his heavy crown.
It felt so hot and tight.
His dear Mama had worn it well,
On her it looked just right.

His wife said, 'Do not worry, dear,
I know your job is new,
but go and find your Happy Place
and work out what to do.'

The garden was his Happy Place,
he'd potter there for hours
with honey bees and birds and trees,
and butterflies and flowers.

One's book belongs to

....

To my sister Maureen who loves to create rhymes.
S. M. B.

To my niece and book lover Evie.
M. B.

Published in 2023 by Welbeck Flame
An imprint of Welbeck Children's Limited,
Part of the Welbeck Publishing Group
Offices in: London – 20 Mortimer Street, London W1T 3JW &
Sydney – 205 Commonwealth Street, Surry Hills 2010

www.welbeckpublishing.com

A CIP catalogue record for this book is available from the British Library.

ISBN 978 1 80338 132 9

Printed by Balto Print in Lithuania

10 9 8 7 6 5 4 3 2 1

His old friend, Tom, the gardener,
said, 'Sire, why do you frown?'
The King replied, 'I've tried and tried,
to wear this heavy crown.'

Said Tom, 'Sit here upon this chair,
we'll have a little chat.
Remember kings do many things
and wear all kinds of hat.'

'You can wear my sunhat,
when you come and weed the path,
and when you get all muddy
wear your shower cap in the bath.'

'A helmet in the lifeboat,
will protect the royal head.
Although your poor old tummy,
may prefer dry land instead.'

'A hard hat on a building site,
bright yellow is the best.
And for health and safety,
you can wear a matching vest.'

'When visiting a factory
making cakes and bread,
you wear a set of overalls,
and a hairnet on your head.'

'Visiting the farmers
is a very special treat.
A wide-brimmed rain-hat on your head,
and wellies on your feet.'

'When visiting the hospital
you must stay nice and clean.
An apron, gloves and cap before
the patients can be seen.'

'You'll have a hat with feathers
to parade in on your horse.
Though sometimes they'll go up your nose,
and make you sneeze, of course.'

'When there is a party,
You can wear a paper crown.
And just to make the children laugh,
You'll wear it upside-down.'

'But sometimes you must wear your crown,
And you will smile and wave.
Your crown is very heavy,
But remember...

...kings are brave.'

'Thank you, Tom', the King said,
'I feel lighter now, by far.
The crown will fit me one day,
Like it fitted dear Mama...'

'But maybe that's enough with
all the king stuff, for today.
The garden path needs weeding.

'Tom, your sunhat if I may.'